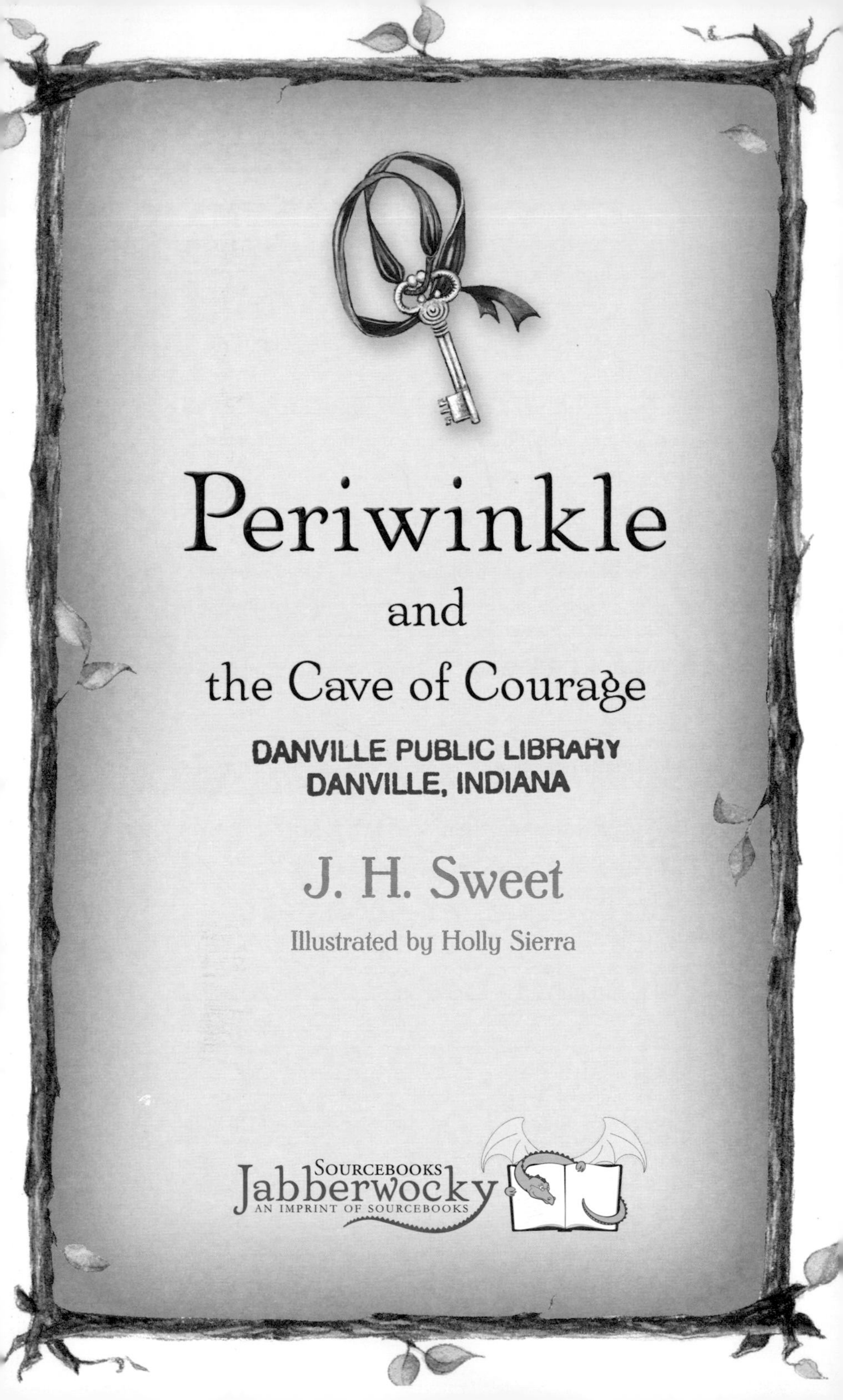

Periwinkle

and

the Cave of Courage

J. H. Sweet

Illustrated by Holly Sierra

SOURCEBOOKS
Jabberwocky
AN IMPRINT OF SOURCEBOOKS

What follows is the original, unedited manuscript directly from the author. It is her vision in its purest form.

Published by Sourcebooks Jabberwocky, an imprint of Sourcebooks, Inc.
P.O. Box 4410, Naperville, Illinois 60567-4410
(630) 961-3900
Fax: (630) 961-2168
www.sourcebooks.com

Cataloging in Publication data is on file with the Publisher.

Printed and bound in the United States of America.
IN 10 9 8 7 6 5 4 3 2 1

To Susie, for courage
and to Kathy, for telling me about
raisin pockets

MEET THE

Periwinkle

NAME:
Vinca Simpson

FAIRY NAME AND SPIRIT:
Periwinkle

WAND:
Elephant's Eyelash

GIFT:
Ability to channel energy from the sun, resistant to heat

MENTOR:
Mrs. Welles, Madam Rose

Cinnabar

NAME:
Helen Michaels

FAIRY NAME AND SPIRIT:
Cinnabar

WAND:
An Aspen Twig

GIFT:
Enhanced abilities at night

MENTOR:
Mrs. Thompson, Madam Finch

FAIRY TEAM

Spiderwort

NAME:
Jensen Fortini

FAIRY NAME AND SPIRIT:
Spiderwort

WAND:
Small, Brilliant Red
Cardinal Feather

GIFT:
Cleverness; the ability
to come up with good ideas
and plans

MENTOR:
Godmother, Madam Chameleon

Rosemary

NAME:
Bailey Richardson

FAIRY NAME AND SPIRIT:
Rosemary

WAND:
Nine Strands of Orangutan
Hair, Triple Braided

GIFT:
An amazing memory

MENTOR:
Mrs. Clark, Madam Chameleon

Inside you is the power to do anything

Marigold and the Feather of Hope, the Journey Begins

Dragonfly and the Web of Dreams

Thistle and the Shell of Laughter

Firefly and the Quest of the Black Squirrel

Spiderwort and the Princess of Haiku

Periwinkle and the Cave of Courage

Cinnabar and the Island of Shadows

Mimosa and the River of Wisdom

Come visit us at fairychronicles.com

Contents

Chapter One

Under the Sycamore Tree

Vinca Simpson was having the best summer of her life. Two weeks before, the adoption paperwork became final, and Vinca officially and legally belonged to her new family. Mr. and Mrs. Martinez were the third foster family Vinca had lived with since her parents passed away when she was five. Now, she was nine years old and had a whole family again, including a new ten-year-old sister named Megan.

The entire family had just returned from a trip to visit Vinca's great-grandfather who lived on an Indian reservation in New Mexico. Since her parents had passed away when

she was so young, Vinca had little opportunity to learn about her family's heritage, so this trip was very important to her.

In addition to learning more about the Native American culture, and meeting Vinca's great-grandfather for the first time, Mr. and Mrs. Martinez had come home with a beautiful piece of pottery and a hand-woven blanket. Megan and Vinca had each purchased brightly colored, handmade bead bracelets.

Being adopted and taking the trip to New Mexico were the highlights of her summer so far, but they weren't the only exciting things going on in Vinca's life. In addition to being just like other girls her age, who were enjoying skating, swimming, and climbing trees in the summer months, she also participated in some other, very important, secret activities.

Vinca was a fairy, and just last month, she went on a very exciting adventure with

several fairy friends. During their mission, the girls helped to rescue the Princess of Haiku from a terrible spell and two ogres possessed by evil spirits. The purpose of fairies was to protect nature and fix problems, which was why Vinca and her friends stayed very busy year round. However, they were not allowed to use fairy magic for trivial matters or to solve simple, everyday problems.

Vinca had been given the fairy spirit of a pink periwinkle flower, and she was called Periwinkle by other fairies. In fairy form, she wore a rosy pink dress made of soft, silky flower petals that came to just above her knees. She also had tiny, feathery pink wings and wore a periwinkle flower barrette to hold back her long dark hair. Periwinkle's wand was one of the most interesting in the fairy realm—an elephant's eyelash. The eyelash was long, dark gray, and slightly curved.

Regular people could not recognize fairies when they saw them. To non-magical people, fairies only appeared to look like their fairy spirits of berries, insects, tiny rodents, flowers, tree blossoms, small lizards, and such like. If Periwinkle's parents happened to see her in fairy form, they would think she was just a normal periwinkle flower. And since standard fairy size was six inches high, Periwinkle would not appear in any way unusual, unless of course it was the dead of winter when periwinkles were not usually in bloom.

Because of her Native American heritage, Periwinkle also had a spirit guide. He took the form of a small snail and most often rode on her shoulder, giving her advice and guidance when needed. However, Periwinkle was the only one who could see her tiny companion and hear his words of wisdom.

Fairies were also given unique gifts relating to their fairy spirits. Periwinkle's special fairy gift was the ability to channel energy from the sun. She soaked up sunshine whenever she could; it gave her strength. Periwinkle also had natural leadership abilities and was good at guiding others. She had a quiet strength and confidence relating to both her fairy spirit and her heritage. This made others trust her good judgment and decisions.

Periwinkle's mentor was a yellow rose fairy called Madam Rose. She was also Mrs. Welles, a social worker in the foster care system, so she was able to arrange for Periwinkle to be away from home frequently to participate in fairy activities.

Periwinkle had received a nut message two days ago from Madam Rose. Nut messages were hollowed-out nuts used for fairy communication. Notes and letters were secreted inside the nuts, which were then

delivered by birds and animals. Madam Rose had arranged for Periwinkle to spend an entire day at a fairy gathering, otherwise known as a Fairy Circle.

The upcoming Fairy Circle was going to be a celebration, and many special guests had been invited. Madam Rose had already telephoned Periwinkle's parents to arrange an early-morning pickup for the all-day outing.

The fairy mentor arrived promptly at eight, as expected. Jensen Fortini, Bailey Richardson, and Helen Michaels were already in Madam Rose's green mini-van.

Jensen was a spiderwort fairy, and she had led their last fairy mission. In fairy form, Spiderwort wore a dark green dress made of long, pointed leaves with bright blue flowers scattered over the bodice and skirt. She had short, wavy, strawberry blond hair, pulled back in a headband covered with tiny spiderwort flowers.

Spiderwort also had tall, sparkling, brilliant blue fairy wings. Her wand was a bright red cardinal feather, and her special fairy gift included cleverness and quick thinking. She was a terrific problem solver, excellent at organizing and planning, and was also very good at things like crossword puzzles, chess, and debate.

Bailey was a rosemary fairy. As a fairy, Rosemary wore a frosty green dress made of short, pine-needle-like leaves with very tiny, creamy, light blue flowers peeking out from between the leaves. She had shoulder-length, light brown curly hair and tiny, pale green wings. Her wand was made of nine triple-braided orangutan hairs.

Rosemary's special fairy gift was an amazing memory. She was able to remember long lists of things, and could often recite whole paragraphs from books after only one reading. And she never forgot important information when studying for school exams.

Rosemary was also the most fragrant of all the fairies and smelled like a mixture of mint and pine trees.

Helen's fairy spirit was that of a cinnabar moth. She had tall, bright red wings with sooty gray striping along the edges. Her fairy dress was made of shimmering, black velvet fuzz, and she carried an enchanted aspen twig for her wand. Cinnabar was a thin, graceful black girl with straight dark hair that came just to her shoulders. She studied ballet and was very elegant in appearance. Even though she had a quiet and reserved personality, she drew attention with her grace and beauty.

For her special fairy gift, Cinnabar was given the ability to function well in the dark. In fact, she excelled at just about everything at night. She could see better, fly better, and had more energy after dark.

The girls were all happy to see one another and chatted together about their

summer fun so far. Periwinkle was anxious to tell her friends about the trip to visit her great-grandfather, and she had brought back bead bracelets for each of them. They thanked her for the lovely gifts and admired the beautiful craftsmanship. The girls all liked to work with beads themselves, but they had never seen beadwork this intricate or delicate.

Rosemary was a little tired and worn out this morning because she had to clean up a brownie mess earlier. The Richardson family had two brownies living in their home. Brownies were boy fairies about seven inches in height. They didn't have wings like girl fairies so they were not able to fly, but they had a very special relationship with many creatures of nature. Animals and birds often helped to carry the brownies whenever they needed to travel.

Brownies liked to live with families, and they sometimes performed chores to be

helpful. However, the boys often got into trouble because they loved to play tricks and cause mischief. If properly rewarded with pastries and milk for helping with tasks such as untangling string, finding lost items, matching up socks from the laundry, and keeping tool drawers organized, the brownies usually kept their pranks under control. However, this summer, Rosemary seemed to be running herself ragged cleaning up after Ryan and Edgar.

Early in the morning, in an attempt to mix up some of the spices in the spice containers, the boys had spilled tarragon, cayenne pepper, thyme, cumin, and garlic salt all over the kitchen counters. Rosemary had to clean up the mess before her parents discovered the mischief. But Ryan and Edgar were only nine years old. Maybe the boys would cause fewer problems when they got a little older. Many brownies were actually very responsible,

despite their mischief. In fact, the brownies had helped the fairies several times on their missions. However, Rosemary did wonder why girls seemed to be so much more mature than boys. She was very puzzled as to why Edgar and Ryan, who were nearly exactly her age, still acted like little hooligans much of the time.

As they drove to Fairy Circle, Madam Rose told the fairies that several brownies would be attending their celebration today, along with trolls, dwarves, leprechauns, and gnomes. The girls were thrilled to hear this. They knew a lot about garden gnomes, and Periwinkle had met a dwarf once, but none of them had ever encountered a troll or a leprechaun before. They talked excitedly about the upcoming party, and the prospect of meeting other magical creatures, while Madam Rose drove down country lanes and through the woods to their Fairy Circle site.

Today's Fairy Circle celebration was taking place under a tall sycamore tree with a massive, gray and white trunk and large, shading leaves. The fairies often met under trees that had special significance to the purpose of their gathering. As they approached the tree, Madam Rose told the girls that sycamore trees were symbolic of strength, courage, and persistence.

Already, many brownies, dwarves, leprechauns, trolls, and gnomes were present. The girls quickly realized that their existing friendship with certain garden gnomes would tell them nothing about their guests today because these were all wood gnomes. They were about ten inches high and wore dark green clothing.

By consulting their fairy handbooks, the fairies found out that wood gnomes differed from garden gnomes in several ways. First of all, wood gnomes had beards, instead of the bushy moustaches that

garden gnomes sported. And they lived in tree houses instead of dugout houses. Their purpose was pretty much the same though: both garden gnomes and wood gnomes were tasked with the job of adding colors to nature and helping to make plants grow.

As Madam Rose went to consult with Madam Toad, the leader of the fairies for this region, the girls flew around the Fairy Circle, visiting with many of their fairy friends including Thistle, Marigold, Lily, Snapdragon, Mimosa, Firefly, Primrose, and Hollyhock.

Primrose and Hollyhock were cousins, and they stayed very close to one another. Since Hollyhock was the only deaf fairy in their group, she sometimes needed a sign language interpreter to converse with others. Even though she could read lips very well, and many of the fairies were learning American Sign Language, she would need a little

help communicating with the many different guests today. Both Primrose and Madam Swallowtail were fluent in sign language.

Periwinkle, Spiderwort, Rosemary, and Cinnabar noticed that many of the other fairies were looking things up in their handbooks. The girls approached Morning Glory and her sister, Skipper, who was a dustywing skipper butterfly fairy. They were looking up trolls. From the handbook, the fairies discovered that trolls were usually four feet high, had eight fingers and eight toes each, could sometimes have more than one head, and slept during the day because they would turn to stone if sunlight touched them. Trolls were also easily confused and had terrible memories.

Most of the trolls in the group today were dressed in loose, comfortable clothing in colors of natural things such as cinnamon, mustard, sage, cranberries, mushrooms, chocolate, asparagus, pumpkins, and celery.

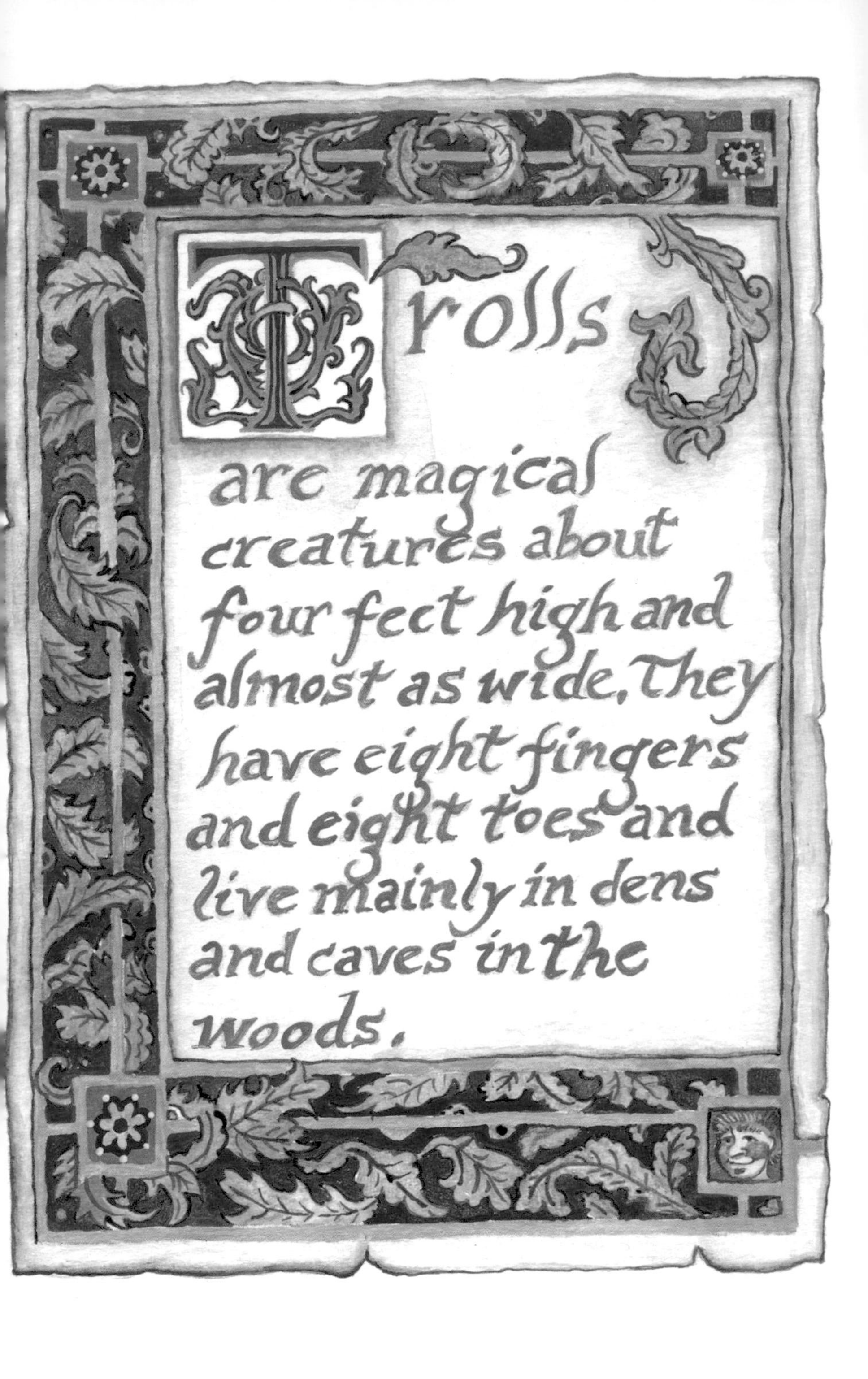
Trolls
are magical creatures about four feet high and almost as wide. They have eight fingers and eight toes and live mainly in dens and caves in the woods.

There was nothing as yet to explain how the trolls could be out in the sunlight today without having turned to stone.

Next, the fairies looked up dwarves in the handbook and found out that dwarves were generally a little shorter than trolls and could be somewhat greedy, often hoarding riches. They were also masters of keeping secrets. In fact, dwarves never even shared their names with anyone, except fellow dwarves.

The fairies already knew about brownies, so they looked up leprechauns next and discovered that leprechauns could fly without wings by means of secret magical shamrocks kept in their pockets. They also found out that leprechauns could appear and disappear at will, and that they were often even greedier than dwarves. Leprechauns were also expert treasure finders, could appear as any color, and were able to change their color whenever they liked.

Looking around the Fairy Circle, the girls saw little groups of leprechauns in many different colors including yellow, blue, orange, purple, and green. The leprechauns were slightly smaller than gnomes, but since they were flying around, it was hard to tell a difference in their sizes compared to gnomes.

Madam June Beetle, Madam Swallowtail, and Madam Chameleon spread out over the Fairy Circle, instructing the younger fairies to visit with their guests and not to stay in their own little groups. This special Fairy Circle had been arranged so that magical creatures of all kinds could get to know one another better.

Spiderwort and Cinnabar eventually got brave enough to approach a group of trolls who grinned happily at them and seemed anxious to visit.

The girls found out that Mother Nature, the guardian of magical creatures, had put a

special *Sunlight Protection Spell* on the trolls, so they could be out in the sunshine for the day and not turn to stone. The fairies also found out that the trolls had brought special pumpkin cookies to the celebration, and were very anxious to have others start enjoying them.

The food at the gathering was quite diverse. In addition to the usual fairy staples of powdered sugar puff pastries, lemon jellybeans, homemade fudge, raspberries, and peanut butter and marshmallow crème sandwiches, the fairies enjoyed many wonderful treats brought by their guests. They had the pumpkin cookies the trolls had made. However, the cookies tasted a little funny, since the trolls had either forgotten or mixed up some of the ingredients. The dwarves had cooked up some pickled eggs and beets, while the leprechauns had baked fancy flying cupcakes. And the brownies had gathered many different kinds of nuts and seeds to

bring to the celebration. The group also drank cider, root beer, lemonade, cranberry juice, coffee, and iced tea.

Periwinkle visited with several of the wood gnomes, who seemed a little more serious and slightly less friendly than the garden gnomes she was used to talking to. The gnomes were very polite, but seemed to prefer to keep to themselves. A couple of them were grumbling about missing work that day and getting behind in their schedules. They were worrying and fretting about how much they were going to have to do the next day to catch up.

Cinnabar was able to visit with a brownie named James whom she had first met a little over a month before. They had corresponded for several weeks through nut messages, and even went on a picnic together two weeks before.

James and his twin brother, John, also known as Donnybrook and Ruckus,

because all brownie twins had nicknames, were granite rock brownies. They were eleven years old, had reddish-brown hair, and wore strings of polished granite chips around their necks.

There were many different kinds of brownies at the party. Brownies got their spirits from earthy things like acorns and river stones, so they were almost as varied and diverse as the fairies. Some of the more common brownie spirits included moss, pinecone, amber, juniper, slate, mushroom, quartz, sand, jasper, and clover.

Brownie Christopher, the leader of the brownies, was also present. He was older than most of the other boys, at fourteen, and was more serious. He stayed mostly to himself and kept a close eye on the other brownies. Christopher felt that his job for the day was to keep brownie mischief in check, so he was very watchful of their activities.

The brownies looked slightly different today than when the girls had seen them before. Their clothes were not nearly as shabby and torn, and most of the boys had obviously combed their hair. It seemed that spending time with fairies was having somewhat of a neatness effect on the brownies.

A few fairies from other regions were also able to attend Fairy Circle today. Madam Oyster and Starfish from the Gulf region had arrived on a blue heron, and Milkweed and Madam Shrew from the far North region had flown in on a spotted owl. They were very happy to join the celebration.

A few purple and blue leprechauns hovering at the edge of the gathering by themselves were grumbling, and one of them said, "It looks like the fairies are too good to talk to us."

Another one nodded and added, "Yeah. Most of the fairies I've met in my life were snobby."

None of the leprechauns bothered to leave their little group to go talk to any of the fairies. They just continued to nod and agree with each other that most fairies were snobs. However, when Snapdragon, Skipper, and Pumpkinwing brought over some pastries and raspberries to share with the group of purple and blue leprechauns, they all visited happily with one another.

After awhile, the leprechauns were completely enchanted with their new fairy friends, and they couldn't resist showing off a little. As the girls watched, the tiny men began changing colors spontaneously to entertain them. Snapdragon and Skipper covered their mouths and giggled as the blue leprechauns changed first to hot pink, then to bright yellow. And Pumpkinwing sat down in the grass, clapping her hands and laughing, as she watched the purple leprechauns change to red, then orange, then green, before turning purple again.

Many of the dwarves had brought their squits to the gathering. Squits were dwarf pets that looked like furry balls. They were about the size of soccer balls and were many different solid colors. There were squits in turquoise, lemon yellow, lilac, orange, bright green, red, and even a black one. In the process of catching invisible air flies, the squits were all bouncing around Fairy Circle like popping popcorn.

However, the fairies knew that it was possible that the squits did not actually exist. Many magical beings commonly thought that squits were a dwarf mind-trick: a distraction technique to keep others from getting a good look at the dwarves' hoarded riches.

Touching squits to see if they were real or not was nearly impossible because the fluffy creatures moved so fast, popping around like firecrackers while chasing air flies. And the dwarves were such good keepers of secrets, they never owned up to any mind-trick, but always acted as though the squits were completely real. Most of the fairies didn't care if they were real or not; they just loved watching the squits bounce around.

One of the lilac squits bounced so fast and furious that he knocked over one of the refreshment tables. His dwarf owner came over to shoo him away from the mess.

Thistle, Primrose, Firefly, and Spiderwort had been watching, and Thistle asked her

friends, "If the squit isn't real, how did he knock over the table?"

The girls thought about this for a few seconds, then Primrose stated, "He must be real."

However, Firefly shrewdly gave her input. "Unless it was dwarf magic that knocked over the table, to confuse us and add weight to the proof of the existence of squits."

The girls all laughed. Mysteries were so much fun!

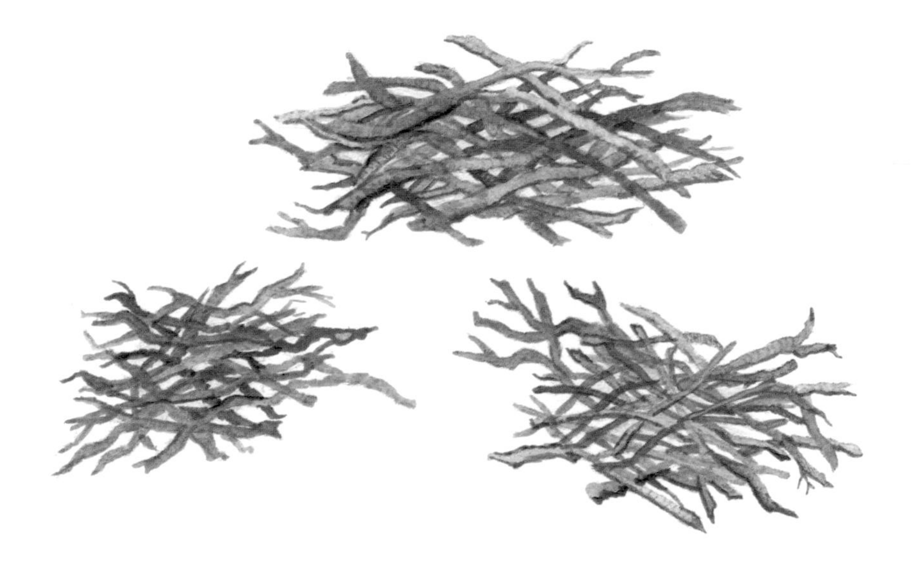

The trolls were keeping very busy at the Fairy Circle. All around the outer edges of the gathering, little piles of leaves, acorns, pinecones, stones, and twigs began to appear. Trolls loved to stack, sort, and pile things. They were very organized. Several of the fairies made a point to admire the work. The praise was met with wide, beaming smiles as the trolls continued to gather, arrange, pat, and separate their stacks and heaps. They very much enjoyed the recognition for their efforts.

Chapter Two

The Challenge

After everyone had visited together for about an hour, and stuffed themselves very full of the goodies, Madam Toad called the meeting to order to describe the reason for their gathering.

The fairy leader looked very beautiful today. She wore a crown of tiny red rose-buds and had small, sparkling, dark green wings. The underskirt and sleeves of her dress were a greenish-brown colour, but her pale green overskirt and bodice sparkled brightly with thousands of tiny moisture droplets.

"Welcome! Welcome, everyone!" she boomed. Madam Toad was a very old and powerful fairy, and was well liked by everyone. The trolls, dwarves, gnomes, brownies, leprechauns, and fairies all listened respectfully as she began to speak. "Mother Nature directed me to call this meeting today."

Even though Madam Toad had met with Mother Nature before, everyone was impressed. Few creatures ever saw Mother Nature. She was very powerful, extremely busy, and often dangerous. And she could take any form she liked. It was never possible to predict when Mother Nature would be in a safe form like a sand drift, echo, shooting star, or dew. Rather, she often took on dangerous states such as lightning, earthquake, blizzard, mudslide, and typhoon.

"I have been instructed to tell you of a challenge we must all participate in," continued Madam Toad. "Not far from here

lies the entrance to the Cave of Courage. The Cave of Courage produces courage for all of mankind. Every one hundred years, the cave must be recharged. This is done by an organized team effort between magical creatures. For this recharging, Mother Nature has chosen a dwarf, a leprechaun, a gnome, a troll, two brownies, and four fairies to participate."

As Madam Toad said this, a burly dwarf stepped forward. He was dressed in dwarf work clothes, which were very much like mining clothes in colors of black, white, and gray.

Next, a leprechaun named Tom flew forward to a position beside the dwarf. Tom had worked with the fairies before in helping to recover the stolen Shell of Laughter last Christmas. He was dressed entirely in orange including his jacket, vest, shirt, trousers, and shoes. Orange was his favorite color; however, today, Tom had

made his hair light blue, for a bit of contrast to his orange attire. He was smiling happily and looked very proud to be chosen for the challenge.

A wood gnome named Mr. Ambertoes joined the group next. He looked very serious and more than a little impatient. He was clearly ready to get on with the task at hand so that he could be getting back to his regular gnome business as quickly as possible. His jacket, pants, hat, and shoes were all dark green.

After Mr. Ambertoes was introduced, James and John stepped forward. They were all smiles, and were very proud to have been selected by Christopher to represent the brownies.

A girl troll named Annie came forward next. She had bushy blond hair and eyebrows, and wore a dress of eggplant purple with a wheat-colored jacket and olive-toned shoes. She tripped on a stick on her way to

join the group and almost fell on her face. But the dwarf caught Annie's arm just in time and helped her land on her knees instead. Evidently, it was pretty common for trolls to stumble because she didn't seem upset at all.

Annie was smiling happily and shook hands with everyone, almost smashing James and John in her eagerness to shake their tiny hands too. They scurried backwards and managed to each grab one of her fingers to shake so they wouldn't be flattened by her large, clumsy, four-fingered hand.

The fairies all waited eagerly and hopefully for Madam Toad to announce who of the fairies would be involved in the challenge. She didn't keep them waiting. "I have decided that Periwinkle, Cinnabar, Spiderwort, and Rosemary will represent the fairies. They did such a good job rescuing the Princess of Haiku last month

that they deserve to participate in another adventure." The girls grabbed each other's hands and bounced up and down with excitement.

Everyone at the Fairy Circle applauded as the assembled team stood together in the center of the group.

"Now, let's go over the rules of the challenge," said Madam Toad. "First, all of the tasks must be completed by nightfall. You will enter the cave and pass from chamber to chamber, working together to complete the tasks. It is very important for you to understand that everyone must participate equally to overcome each obstacle. Teamwork is an important part of courage and is crucial in the recharging process of the cave."

The members of the group nodded in understanding at one another as Madam Toad went on. "At the end of the day, when you reach the last chamber and complete

the final task, Mother Nature will award a prize to one member of the group. She will grant any request to the one who has shown the most bravery and courage. So, while you participate in the challenge, think about what you might like to select as a gift from Mother Nature, if you are

chosen as the most courageous.

"Instructions for each task will be located on the door of each chamber of the cave. Remember, the primary goal is to complete the obstacle course to recharge the cave. This is a friendly competition. You will be required to help one another

along the way. We have worked successfully together before. Remember, you must all stay together, participate in every task, and complete everything."

As Madam Toad finished giving instructions, the members of the group started thinking about teamwork, courage, and what they would select as a prize if chosen as the most brave.

Chapter Three

A Puzzle

As the entire group of fairies, brownies, trolls, gnomes, dwarves, and leprechauns proceeded to escort the participants to the mouth of the Cave of Courage, which was only about fifty feet from the majestic, towering sycamore tree, Periwinkle concentrated on soaking up the sun's rays for strength, since it was unlikely that she would encounter any sunshine inside the cave.

The entrance to the Cave of Courage was narrow, not much more than a small opening between two large gray stones, and otherwise unremarkable. The plain and insignificant

appearance of the entrance made it hard for the group to believe that this was the source of all courage on earth.

The mission participants proceeded inside carefully, and a little apprehensively, since they had no idea what they might encounter first.

As they traveled through a narrow, dark section at the beginning of the cave, the fairies all whispered, "*Fairy light*," to make the tips of their wands glow softly. Periwinkle's spirit guide spoke encouraging words in her ear to help calm the butterfly flutterings in her stomach.

The first chamber of the cave contained a large, round, silver door with an egg timer built into the exact center of the door.

Periwinkle took the lead and approached the door, reading aloud the instructions etched over the top of it: "*Solve the puzzle before time runs out and the door shrinks too small.*"

Solve the puzzle before
time runs out and the
door shrinks too small.

As soon as she said this, a line of letters appeared on the silver door just above the egg timer.

The puzzle was a series of mixed-up letters of the alphabet that didn't make any sense. Above each of the letters was a small line waiting to be filled in with the correct letter. There were only two words in the puzzle. The first word was very long and contained three hyphens, and the second word was very short. The puzzle also contained four clues: the first and last letters of each of the two words were already filled in.

As the egg timer on the door set itself to three minutes and began timing, the smooth silver door began slowly shrinking.

W _ _ _ _ _ - _ _ _ - _ _ _ _ _ _ -

Q C J P X L F H L L X X D G X

_ _ _ _ R S _ _ _ H

O C K X J U K H M O

Very quickly, Periwinkle said, "Spiderwort, take over! You are the best puzzle solver in the group."

Pulling a pencil out of her pocket, Spiderwort flew forward to face the puzzle.

"It's a cryptogram," she said. "The strange letters underneath stand for letters of the alphabet—this is like breaking a secret code. We have four of the letters. We can fill in the other places where they fit, then work on other letter combinations."

However, when she did this, only one more letter of the puzzle was revealed:

W _ _ _ _ _ - _ _ _ - _ _ _ _ _ _ -
Q C J P X L   F H L   L X X D G X

H _ _ _ R   S _ _ _ H
O C K X J   U K H M O

"Okay, now we'll look at letter combinations. The double Xs could be Es."

Spiderwort paused for a moment, then added, "And the last word could be Smith."

W _ _ _ E _ - _ I _ - _ E E _ _ E -
Q C J P X L   F H L   L X X D G X

H _ M E R   S M I T H
O C K X J   U K H M O

The puzzle was starting to take shape. Unfortunately, Spiderwort was stuck and time was running out. Already, over a minute had passed; and the door was looking doubtfully small for a troll, or even a dwarf, to fit through. "Oh no! Oh no!" she fretted. "I'm stumped."

The other members of the group tried to give input. James, John, and Tom were trying to help, but only managed to say, "Um...Umm...Uh..."

Annie was confusing everyone by shouting words and names that couldn't possibly

be the first word. "Richard Smith! Blacksmith! Jeremiah Smith!"

"Stop, Annie!" cried Periwinkle, frustrated. "Those are all wrong!"

Mr. Ambertoes, Cinnabar, and Rosemary were studying the puzzle with intense concentration and muttering words they thought might fit in, but they never hit on anything correct.

Annie had started shouting again and was once more confusing everyone, including herself.

Periwinkle noticed that the dwarf was acting strangely. He was pacing back and forth, grumbling, and stomping his feet. He looked very mad. Time was almost out.

Even Periwinkle's spirit guide had no idea the answer to the puzzle. He shook his head when she looked at him. "I can't believe we are going to fail in our first task," she said. "This is terrible!"

Just as the timer was counting down the

last five seconds, and the door was looking positively too small for use by either the dwarf or Annie, the dwarf said loudly, "Warfen-Kin-Neeble-Hamer Smith!"

He was right!

The timer stopped at one second to go, and the letters of the puzzle magically filled themselves in. Then the puzzle disappeared, as the door stopped shrinking and slowly swung open.

The dwarf sat down cross-legged on the floor of the cave and shook his head. He still looked angry and upset, even though the others of the group were cheering.

"You solved the puzzle!" cried Periwinkle. "What's wrong? Why are you so angry?"

"I'll tell you why I'm angry!" he said loudly. The dwarf paused for a few seconds, took a deep breath, and then added more calmly, "The puzzle is my name. Dwarves never share their names. They are secret. We only share our names with other dwarves."

"But, why?" asked Rosemary. "It's a very interesting name."

"Well, for one thing, dwarf names are so long that no one can ever remember them correctly."

"I can remember it," replied Rosemary, and she proceeded to repeat his name carefully, and correctly. "Warfen-Kin-Neeble-Hamer Smith."

The dwarf smiled and responded, "But you may be the only one who can remember it. It's kind of insulting for people to almost never get your name right."

The others sat watching him carefully to see if he was still upset at having to reveal his name. After a few moments, he added, "Not sharing our names also adds to the dwarf mystique. We are supposed to be experts and masters of keeping secrets. If we are forced to reveal our names, we might not be held in very high esteem with regards to our secret-keeping abilities.

Then where would we be?"

The others nodded understandingly, and Annie said, "It's a lovely name." Then she added, "King-Hammer-Smith of Keeble-Worf."

"No, Annie!" said Rosemary, exasperatedly. "It's Warfen-Kin-Neeble-Hamer Smith!"

Rosemary was silent with the others for a minute. Then she had an idea. "What if we just call you Mr. Smith? Then no one else would know that you had revealed your whole secret name to us. And Mr. Smith is simple enough that everyone here can probably remember it and get it right."

The rest of the group looked sideways at Annie, who was muttering, "Mr. Smith, Mr. Smith, Mr. Smith…" under her breath, trying to memorize the name.

The dwarf smiled and nodded. "That would be highly acceptable," he said. "Thank you."

The others breathed a sigh of relief. Then they all either climbed or flew through the door, pulling Annie through last of all because she sort of got stuck in the shrunken door. When the tugging finally caused Annie to pop through the doorway like a cork, she almost squashed Tom and Mr. Ambertoes.

At this point, everyone was a little frustrated at having to drag a troll along. However, Annie was smiling happily. She was having fun with her new friends and was very much looking forward to the next task.

Chapter Four

Treasures

The next chamber they entered was piled full of golden coins and jewelry. Their eyes nearly popping out of their heads, Tom and Mr. Smith were speechless. There were a few oohs, aahs, and soft whistles from the other group members; but otherwise, the challenge participants remained silent.

Many of the pieces of gold jewelry had sparkling rubies, emeralds, opals, diamonds, sapphires, and pearls set into them. There were bracelets, rings, brooches, earrings, pendants, and even crowns.

At the far end of the chamber was a square, solid-emerald door with a large, glittering diamond doorknob. The instructions etched above the emerald door read, *"Select one item each, and one item only."*

James, John, Cinnabar, Periwinkle, Rosemary, Spiderwort, Annie, and Mr. Ambertoes quickly picked up one gold coin each and approached the emerald door. They stood waiting patiently for Tom and Mr. Smith to decide.

The dwarf carefully looked over everything in the chamber and finally selected

an ornate bracelet set with pearls and rubies. He came to stand by the others and turned his back on the rest of the treasure, looking up at the door, hoping for it to open, and trying not to turn around to look again at the rest of the hoard.

Tom flew around in circles, sweating a great deal, and looking a little wild-eyed.

After a few minutes, Periwinkle's spirit guide reminded her that they needed to hurry to complete the challenge all in one day. "Hurry, Tom!" she said. "We are running out of time."

Tom flew even faster, sweating more and more, and turned an even brighter shade of orange. But he couldn't seem to make a decision.

"Do you want us to choose something for you?" asked Cinnabar. The fairies and brownies were actually getting a bit tired holding the heavy coins.

"No! No!" cried Tom.

He finally landed and picked up an enormous ring of white gold that looked as though it might have belonged to an ogre king. The ring featured a giant sapphire with two huge diamonds set on either side of it. The piece was so large that Tom slipped it over his head to carry the ring around his neck. Adorned in this manner, the leprechaun looked as though he were wearing a very expensive, and fancy, dog collar. As Tom had finally selected, the sparkling emerald door swung open, and they all passed into the next chamber.

While making her way through the door, Annie accidentally bumped into Cinnabar and Rosemary, causing them to drop their coins. The girls quickly retrieved the coins and put some distance between themselves and the clumsy troll.

"I wish I could take the emerald door," Tom said, breathlessly, as he passed through the doorway.

The next chamber they entered was very dull in comparison to the one piled with treasure. Although it contained a golden door, the room was very small and had only a stone well situated in the center.

There was very little space for them to move about, so the group formed a circle around the well while Periwinkle flew over to read the instructions above the golden door: *"Drop the treasure into the well to retrieve the key to the door."*

The fairies, brownies, and gnome immediately tossed their coins into the well. Annie tried to do the same, but missed with her first toss and had to hunt down the coin to toss it again. Mr. Smith paused, and sighed a little, before he threw in the pearl and ruby bracelet.

Then everyone looked expectantly at Tom, who looked horrified. "Oh, no!" he cried. "No way!" he added firmly. "I'll never find another ring like this." They all

just looked at him. He was almost crying, shaking his head in disbelief and trembling. "I can't. I just can't," he whimpered.

Annie spoke up quickly. "I have another golden treasure in my pocket. I'll give it to you if you will toss the ring into the well."

Tom thought about this for a few moments. He really didn't have a choice. They had to get the key to open the door.

He slowly flew to hover above the well. Heaving and hoisting the heavy ring over his head, and closing his eyes, he dropped it in. Then he flew backwards until he bumped up against the wall behind him. Leaning flat against the wall, and breathing hard, Tom had turned a milky orange color that was mostly white, with barely an orange tinge left. Tossing the ring was the hardest thing he had ever had to do.

The others were very sympathetic. As everyone expressed concern and told Tom how brave they all thought he was, a rope

ascended from the center of the well. A small bucket attached to the bottom of the rope contained a golden key.

Mr. Ambertoes took the key and unlocked the door. Before they passed through the doorway, Tom and the others looked expectantly at Annie. However, Annie just looked confused, and didn't understand why everyone was staring at her. So Periwinkle reminded her. "Annie, you said you would give Tom a golden treasure in your pocket if he dropped the ring."

"Oh, yes," Annie said, smiling. She then reached into her dress pocket and pulled out a handful of golden raisins.

Tom almost choked with disappointment. "What is this?" he cried.

"Golden raisins!" Annie exclaimed happily. "All trolls have a raisin pocket. Trolls just love raisins. But I love golden raisins best. They are made from white grapes, instead of purple or red ones, and I think

they have a better flavor."

Tom looked very disgusted. However, the others were all smiling.

"That's interesting that all trolls like raisins," said Spiderwort, "because all fairies like lemon jellybeans."

"And all brownies like pastries and milk," added John.

Tom was clearly upset, and getting impatient, because he added snappily, "And all leprechauns like coffee ice cream. So what? Can we get going now? We're wasting time!"

They filed through the door quietly. Even though Annie was very nice, no one in the group had a very high opinion of her. She didn't really seem to fit in. They were all silently wishing that they could complete the rest of the tasks without her interference.

Annie couldn't understand why Tom was so upset. In fact, she was very confused. To her, golden raisins were a treasure.

Chapter Five

The Snake

The next section of the cave was slightly larger than the chamber containing the well. A lavender-colored, padded-silk door, which looked a lot like a giant cushion, occupied one corner of the room. A rattlesnake sat in another corner of the chamber. He hissed at the visitors as they entered.

The group made a wide berth around the snake and looked at one another, a little confused, wondering what they were supposed to do. Periwinkle flew to the top of the door to read the instructions: *"Retrieve the key from the end of the tunnel without touch-*

ing feet, hands, or wings on the walls, floor, or ceiling of the tunnel."

"What tunnel?" asked Mr. Smith.

James and John were kneeling down, looking into a small hole just a few feet from where the rattlesnake was curled up hissing at them. "This tunnel," they both said in unison.

"The hole is very small," added James.

"And very dark," said Cinnabar, landing beside him and peering inside the narrow tunnel.

Periwinkle said, "Cinnabar, you are able to navigate well in the dark, and you are the most graceful and coordinated of all of us. Can you fly in and retrieve the key?"

"Not without bumping my wings," Cinnabar said fretfully. "I wish I could, but it's too narrow. I don't think it will work."

Tom tried to use leprechaun magic, and Mr. Smith tried to use dwarf magic, to entice the key out of the tunnel. Unfortu-

nately, as hard as they tried, they could not attract the key towards them. They could hear it rattling around, trying to come to them, but it was no use.

"The key must be tied with something," said Tom.

Mr. Smith agreed, nodding.

Annie knelt down next to the tunnel. The others thought she just wanted to look inside. Periwinkle happened to be watching and shouted just in time, "No, Annie, don't!"

Annie had started to reach inside the tunnel with her large, clumsy hand. "I thought I might be able to reach the key without touching the walls, floor, or ceiling," she said, sheepishly.

A little off to one side, James and John were having a discussion with one another.

Tom, Mr. Smith, and Mr. Ambertoes were talking about rigging a wire, or something like a wire, to try to retrieve the key.

But none of them had a wire. And the fairies had not learned enough magic yet, on their own, to be able to use their wands to get the key. The fairy handbook always referred young fairies to their mentors when they had questions about wand tricks.

James and John finished their discussion and approached the others, and James said, "I think we have a good plan. I will ask the rattlesnake to take me and Cinnabar into the tunnel to retrieve the key."

At first, the others didn't say anything. They just stared. No one had ever heard of brownies or fairies riding around on dangerous, poisonous snakes.

James shuffled his feet and glanced at Cinnabar nervously. He cleared his throat and explained further. "It's true that brownies don't usually ride on snakes, and we seldom go out of our way to talk to rattlesnakes, but we do have a strong connection to all animals, even reptiles."

"You're brilliant," said Cinnabar, admiringly. "The snake doesn't have feet, hands, or wings, so he's a perfect choice to enter the tunnel." James blushed a little at her words, stuffing his hands into his pockets and looking away. The others agreed with Cinnabar.

"It is a good plan," said Periwinkle, "but be careful."

James approached the rattlesnake cautiously and spoke to the creature calmly, explaining their need for help. He returned to the group a few moments later, smiling, with the slithering snake following him. James told the others, "He is glad to help us. No brownies have ever asked him for help before."

Cinnabar approached the snake and lifted her leg over his body to straddle him just behind his head. She bent her knees and tucked in her feet so they wouldn't be in danger of touching the walls or floor of the tunnel.

James told her, "I will ride behind you and hold your wings still, to keep them from touching the ceiling." He then got onto the snake behind Cinnabar and carefully grasped the tops of her wings, bending them slightly towards him.

The rattlesnake could tell that they were ready and immediately slithered into the dark tunnel, his underbelly scales making only the smallest of scratching sounds in the soft sandy earth of the cave floor.

The other members of the group barely had time to worry about their two friends, riding into a dark tunnel on the back of a rattlesnake, when the snake returned safely with Cinnabar and James. They were both smiling, and Cinnabar was clutching a tiny pewter key tied with a purple silk ribbon.

She was blushing a little because while James had held her wings with one hand, he had put his other arm around her waist to help steady her as they rode on the snake.

James and Cinnabar jumped off the rattlesnake and thanked him for his help. Periwinkle took the key, congratulating them, and flew up to unlock the door. Everyone else in the room also thanked the snake, but Annie almost stepped on him in her eagerness to thank him. He hissed at her as he slithered away, toward the door leading to the well chamber.

Chapter Six

Hard Work

The next part of the cave was very large, and was completely filled with beautiful crystals. The walls, ceiling, and even the floor were covered with many different types of colored crystals. However, even though the stones sparkled brightly, the colors of the crystals were somewhat faded.

A small wooden door with a brass doorknob sat at the opposite end of the crystal-filled room. Above the door, the instructions read, *"Recolor the crystals to recharge them."*

Mr. Ambertoes was already rolling up his sleeves. "This will be hard work," he told his

friends. "And I need your help to complete the work quickly enough to move on. Doing the task by myself would take a couple of days."

The gnome scratched his chin and furrowed his brow in deep thought. Then he said, "I am going to teach each of you a gnome magic colorization technique, and I am going to give each of you a magic mushroom spore. I will put a spore into one of your pockets. You must keep it in your pocket while you work. The spore will help you work faster, and the magic of the spore will make the coloring of the crystals more permanent."

Mr. Ambertoes reached into one of his jacket pockets and pulled out a pinch of tiny mushroom spores, too small for even the fairies or brownies to see. He then carefully put one spore into each of their pockets. Tom steered Mr. Ambertoes away from the jacket pocket where he kept his

magical shamrock, and made him put the spore into his left vest pocket instead.

Then Mr. Ambertoes proceeded to teach each of them a technique to add pigment to a particular color of crystal. First, he told Spiderwort, "For the light blue crystals, stand on your left foot and say the word *jiggy-jog* three times."

Mr. Ambertoes instructed John next. "Sit cross-legged with your hands over your ears and say *wee-yi-bah* to color the dark red ones."

Then Mr. Ambertoes taught Tom to color the yellow ones. "Touch your toes and say *apoof*, twice."

James, Mr. Smith, and the rest of the fairies all received similar instructions to work on a particular color of crystal including green, pink, dark blue, gold, and purple.

Lastly, Mr. Ambertoes tried to give Annie the most simple crystal color to work on, the orange ones, in the hopes

that she would be able to perform the magic correctly. "Just close your eyes and say *buttered brisket*," he said.

Mr. Ambertoes then began to move quickly all over the crystal chamber, while performing complicated twirls, backbends, handstands, and jumps, all the while muttering words that sounded mostly like nonsense. None of the others had ever known that wood gnomes were so acrobatic.

Soon, brightly colored crystals began appearing all over the chamber. The stones were getting expertly recharged under Mr. Ambertoes' exceptional skill, and the hard work of everyone else.

Unfortunately, Annie was having great difficulty, and everyone was becoming very frustrated with her. She had started saying mutton and brisket, instead of buttered brisket, and she kept opening her eyes to look at her work. So the crystals she was trying to recolor were turning out orange-

spotted, instead of orange. Mr. Ambertoes kept sighing heavily, and coming after her to fix her mistakes.

Finally, Tom suggested that she sit in the corner and let them finish, so she would not be making any more work for them. Sad, and frustrated with herself, Annie went to sit in the corner of the chamber.

About an hour later, they finally finished. Mr. Ambertoes surveyed the work, breathing a little hard, stretching his back, and praising everyone.

The wooden door swung open a few moments after they finished, and the group made their way towards it, anxious to enter the next chamber.

As they passed Annie, still sitting in her corner, Mr. Ambertoes suddenly stopped short. James and John ran into the backs of his legs. The gnome was staring at a crystal directly in front of Annie. The stone was a deep, intense shade of orange,

and was, in fact, the most beautiful and brilliant orange crystal he had ever seen. The stone looked exactly like the glowing sun on an orange sunset kind of day.

Annie had been working for the last hour on the same crystal, trying desperately to get it right. She had more than succeeded.

"Wow!" said Mr. Ambertoes. "I don't know what to say. That color is perfect. No gnome could have done better."

Annie smiled happily and stood up to join the others trekking into the next chamber.

Chapter Seven

The Final Door

Everyone was a little tired as they entered the final chamber of the Cave of Courage. This one was very small, almost the size of an elevator, with metal walls. The tiny room had a large, tarnished copper door on one side. The door was a rusty, orange-brown color with green streaks. Above the rusty door was etched the question, *"Who among you has shown the most courage?"*

The group all sat in a little circle to give input and discuss the question.

Tom spoke up right away, saying, "I think

it was extremely brave of Mr. Smith to reveal his name to us."

The dwarf responded, "But it took a lot of courage for you to toss away a treasure. Giving up something that valuable must have been very difficult." Everyone in the room was nodding.

Cinnabar chimed in next. "I think it was very brave of James to talk to the rattlesnake, and to be able to trust the snake to help us."

James gave his input as well. "And it was also brave to face the dark of the tunnel." Everyone continued to nod. No one disagreed with anything that had been said so far.

Spiderwort spoke next. "It took a lot of courage to take on the crystal recolorization. That was an amazing amount of hard work for Mr. Ambertoes to complete in such a short time. He is also a good teacher."

Mr. Ambertoes didn't say anything, but

looked down, pleased that someone noticed he did good work and gave good instructions. Not many people ever noticed, or thought to comment on, the hard work of gnomes.

Periwinkle thought over everything that had been said. However, her spirit guide was whispering urgently in her ear. "Don't let them give an answer yet. Think about everything, and think about what courage actually is."

After everyone had been silent for several minutes, Periwinkle addressed the group. "I don't think we have hit on the answer yet. It is true that it took great courage to share something personal, to give away something valuable, to ask for help and trust another, to face darkness, and to work hard and long to accomplish a task.

"But what is courage?" she continued. "Patience, generosity, tolerance, and understanding are all kinsman to courage. Working

~Courage~
Respect and trust
others, have patience,
learn tolerance, work
as a team, ask for help,
face darkness, work
hard, and try again
when you fail...

together, we accomplished what one alone could not. If all of us had not been present, and combined our efforts, we would not have been able to complete everything and make the journey through the entire cave. Each and every one of us was brave, courageous, and worked hard today." The others listened carefully to what Periwinkle said, and they all nodded in agreement.

Periwinkle finished her speech by saying, "There is someone among us who has all of the qualities related to courage, a person who is generous, patient, tolerant, and understanding—someone who had the bravery to try again, and keep trying, even after failing."

Annie was looking down at her hands, frowning, and thinking hard about who was the bravest of her new friends. She thought and thought. All of them were hardworking, courageous, and better at everything than she was. She really couldn't decide

who she thought was best: James, John, Mr. Ambertoes, Tom, Mr. Smith, Spiderwort, Rosemary, Cinnabar, or Periwinkle. She just couldn't decide.

Annie finally realized that the others had been silent for quite some time, and she looked up. They were all smiling at her, even Tom. And she nearly fainted with shock when Periwinkle faced the door and announced loudly, "Annie is the bravest and has shown the most courage!"

Chapter Eight

Courage

The room they were in actually was an elevator, which began moving as soon as Periwinkle had given the answer. And the conveyance took their breath away as it rose very fast. After about a minute, the lift stopped suddenly, and the copper door slid silently open. Sunlight streamed into the elevator, almost blinding the occupants. However, they were even more stunned to hear the roaring cheers of the crowd awaiting them.

Annie tripped as she ran out of the elevator. Mr. Smith helped her up, and she continued on her way, undaunted, throwing

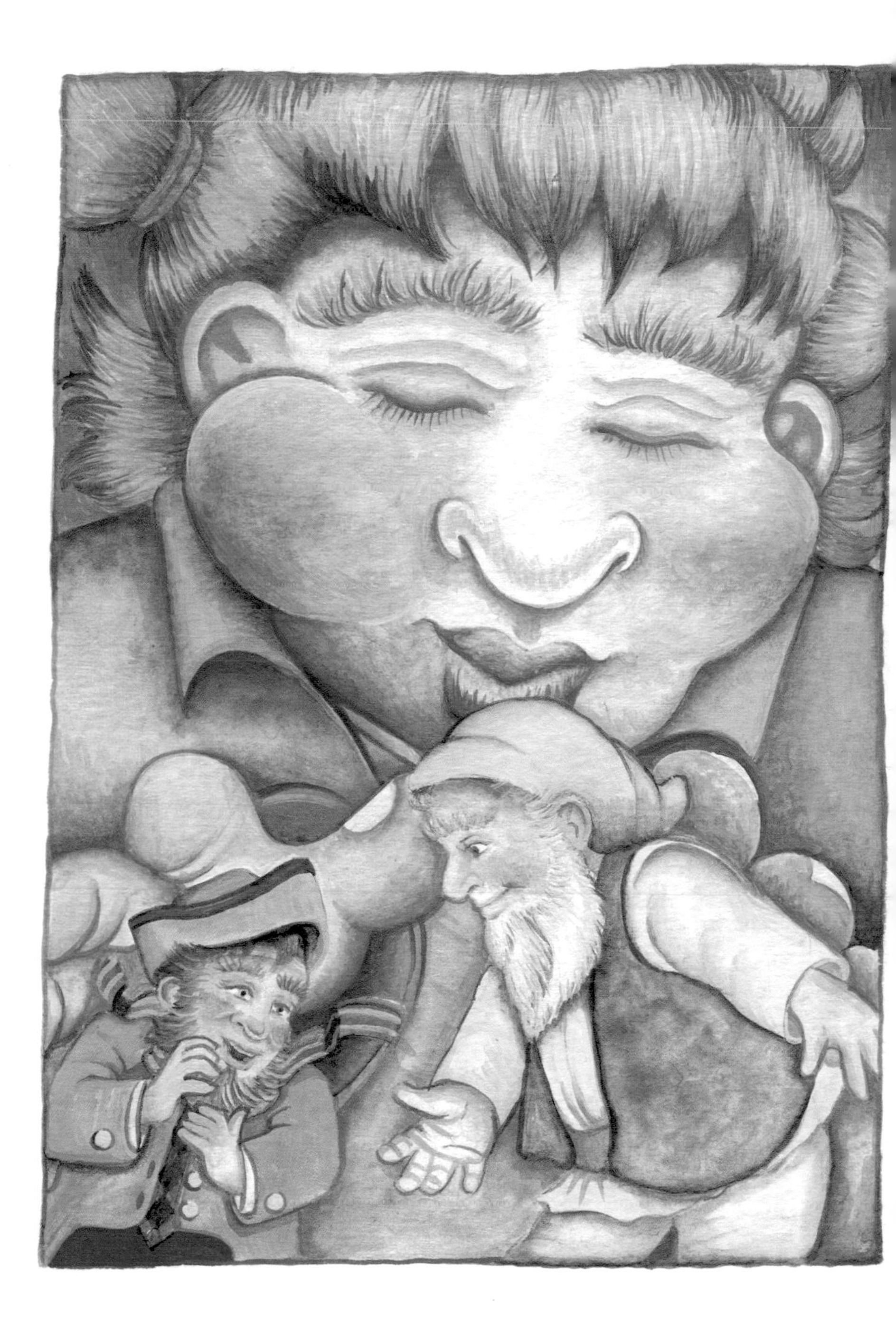

herself into the crowd, hugging everyone she could get her hands on—mainly dwarves, leprechauns, and her troll friends. And she managed to plant kisses on the foreheads of several rather stoic wood gnomes. She was so happy.

Everyone was still cheering loudly when Madam Toad began speaking. "We have a winner of the challenge! Annie has shown the most courage!

"Of course, everyone must have worked together very effectively as a team to complete the tasks," added Madam Toad, "or you would all still be inside the cave. Mother Nature intended this to be an exercise to promote inter-magical-creature-cooperation. I'd say you have all done her very proud today."

Again, the clapping and cheering was very loud as Madam Toad went on. "The courage each of you showed in the cave included the ability to share personal things, to give away treasured belongings,

to ask for help, to trust others, to face darkness, to work hard, and to keep trying even when you failed. Meeting the challenge and completing all of the tasks has successfully recharged the Cave of Courage for another one hundred years."

There was more cheering and applause as Madam Toad paused in her speech. Then she added, "Mother Nature will be here in a few minutes to award the prize." The crowd fell silent as everyone looked around a little apprehensively. Many of the group were afraid of Mother Nature's power, and with good reason.

Madam Toad went on. "I hope you also realize that this has been an exercise in tolerance, and in learning respect for each other. And we must always strive to overcome incorrect perceptions of one another.

"For example, there are some who think that trolls are simply clumsy and confused all of the time. And others believe that

fairies are standoffish and look down on their fellow creatures."

The trolls and fairies were looking around them, wondering who might be thinking these things. The dwarves, brownies, leprechauns, and gnomes all remained silent.

Then Madam Toad continued. "Also, some believe that dwarves are so secretive that they must be untrustworthy. Still others think brownies are so mischievous that they are irresponsible and always up to no good. It is also commonly believed that leprechauns are so greedy, they cannot look beyond a bit of gold to help someone in a time of need. While others have the idea that gnomes are so focused on their work that they do not bother to take the time to get to know anyone else.

"I hope each of you realize that these perceptions are false," added the fairy leader. "We must continue to work together, always helping one another and trusting in each other."

As Madam Toad finished speaking, Mother Nature arrived, and everyone breathed a sigh of relief. She was in rainbow form. The shimmering smooth colors of the rainbow dipped out of the clouds and hovered over them while a soft, sweet breeze caressed the golden rays of late afternoon sunshine slanting through the tree limbs.

The faces of the gathering were alight and glowing, waiting for Mother Nature to speak to them and award the prize. When she spoke, her voice was very earthy and rich, and sounded like a combination of music and wind with a little low thunder mixed in. "Congratulations! And thank you!" she said. "The Cave of Courage has been recharged for all of mankind for the next one hundred years."

There were plenty of grins, and many in the group applauded lightly. However, the crowd restrained itself from any exu-

berant cheering because they wanted to show plenty of respect for Mother Nature.

"Annie, step forward," instructed Mother Nature.

Annie came forward eagerly, and this time didn't trip.

"What will you select as a prize for showing the most courage inside the cave?" Mother Nature asked.

Annie had been going over this in her mind. She knew exactly what she wanted to ask for, but she wanted to make sure she got it right, so she was rehearsing what she wanted to say.

Mother Nature waited patiently as Annie nodded to herself, going over the words in her head. After nearly two minutes, Annie had rehearsed the words five times and finally spoke, slowly and carefully. "A lifetime supply of golden raisins for everyone here."

There was mixed applause, and some

groans, as several of the leprechauns buried their heads in their hands and few of the dwarves shook their heads sadly. Their choices would have been much different and would have involved lots of gold and jewels.

However, the majority of the group was very happy. The fairies, brownies, and gnomes were all smiling. Several of the leprechauns, many of the dwarves, and all of the trolls were grinning and applauding her choice. And all around the gathering, buckets and bins filled with golden raisins began magically appearing.

The group fell silent again as Mother Nature spoke her final words. "You will each receive information on how to request a re-supply of the raisins when they run out." Then she added, "I am very proud of you all. The courage you showed was remarkable. Remember what you have learned today. You are strongest as a team and can accomplish more than you ever

imagined. Have respect, patience, and tolerance for one another. Continue to share, help, trust, face darkness, work hard, and try again when you fail. These things are all part of having courage."

Then the rainbow simply disappeared, and they were left with brilliant blue sky and glittering sunshine.

The new friends all took a long time to say goodbye to one another, and resolved to keep in touch with each other through nut messages and magic.

Periwinkle, Cinnabar, Spiderwort, and Rosemary all piled into Madam Rose's green mini-van. But they were mostly quiet on the trip home, thinking about the Cave of Courage and eating their golden raisins.

The End

Fairy Fun

Annie's Pumpkin Cookie Recipe

400°F
8–10 minutes

2 cups shortening
3 cups granulated sugar
2 eggs
1 twenty-ounce can crushed pineapple in heavy syrup (do not drain)
1 teaspoon vanilla
7 cups flour
2 teaspoons baking soda
1 teaspoon salt
½ teaspoon nutmeg

In a large mixing bowl, combine shortening, sugar, eggs, and vanilla. Beat by hand until well blended. Stir in pineapple with juice. In separate bowl blend flour, soda, salt, and nutmeg. Add to first mixture and stir until well blended.

Drop each teaspoonful on a lightly greased cookie sheet. Bake at 400°F for eight to ten minutes or until there is no imprint when lightly touched.

This makes quite a lot, since trolls tend to bake big batches. You can cut the recipe in half if you like. And even though Annie forgot to add pumpkin to her Pumpkin Cookie Recipe, these cookies are still very good, if you like pineapple.

Be sure to get permission from your parents to cook in the kitchen, and make sure a grownup helps when using sharp instruments and hot appliances.

Cryptograms

A cryptogram is a word puzzle and also a fun way to send messages to others in a secret code. Cryptograms were originally used by Spartan armies in fifth century B.C. as a way to send messages between soldiers without the enemy knowing what they were saying. But now, thousands of years later, the puzzles are used as a way to challenge people's thinking.

Cryptograms are made by replacing letters in a word or sentence with other letters to disguise them. For example, a cryptogram code can change the letter C to D, the letter A to F, and the letter T to G. To spell the word "cat" using the cryptogram code, you would write DFG. This may sound a bit confusing, but once you get the hang of it, it can be quite fun!

Try creating a cryptogram puzzle for your friends to solve. Start by writing the entire alphabet on a piece of paper. Next, write the letter A underneath the letter B. Write the letter B underneath the letter C. Write the letter C underneath the letter D, and so on. When you get to the end of the alphabet, write the letter Z underneath the letter A. Now you have your original "real" alphabet and

your secret code alphabet. When you want to write a message to one of your friends, look at the letter you need in the top line, but write the letter that's underneath it in the bottom line. For example, if you wanted to write the name Periwinkle, you would write QFSJXJOLMF. Try it with your name and try creating your own cryptogram code!

How to Grow a Bowl of Crystals

Please remember, before trying to grow your own crystals or before doing any other experiments ever, to talk to your parents, get their permission, and have them help you along the way!

Things you will need:

½ cup of Epsom salt (sold in the medicine aisle of your local grocery store)

½ cup of hot water (not boiling, just hot)

A spoon for stirring

A bowl your parents are willing to let you grow crystals in

A refrigerator or counter space

This is a really easy and simple way to grow crystals. Here is what you do: Take the ½ cup of Epsom salt and pour it into the bowl. Then, very carefully and with your parents' help, take the hot water and pour it into the bowl. Now stir the salt and water together.

Then, take the bowl and put it in the refrigerator. In three hours, you will have your very own crystals. Depending on what type of bowl you used, the crystals will be different. Use differently shaped

bowls and make different crystals. If you are having trouble getting the crystals out of the bowl because they are delicate, put something hard on the bottom of the bowl (like a silver dollar) for them to grow on.

There are many different kinds of crystals that can be grown in your house and, believe it or not, you can even grow crystals with different colors. To learn more, ask your science teacher or do research with your parents on the internet.

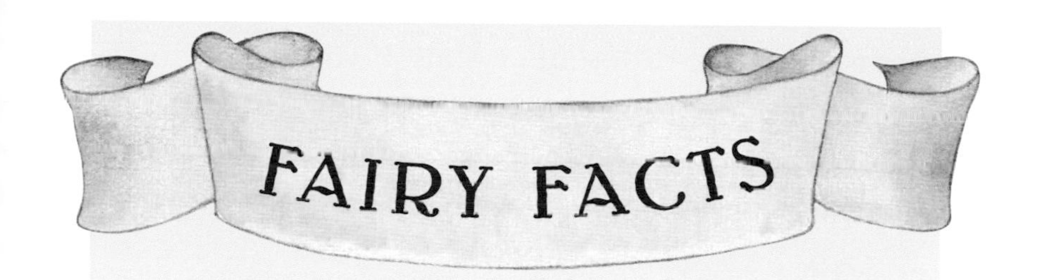

Mammoth Cave National Park

Mammoth Cave National Park is located in central Kentucky. More than 367 miles of the cave have been explored and charted, which makes it the largest mapped cave system in the world. It also means that if you walked a mile a day in the cave, it would take you more than a year to see all of the cave that has been charted by explorers. Or, if you really want to see how big Mammoth Cave is, just go look at a map of the United States. The amount of area that has been explored in Mammoth Cave, if you stretched it out in a straight line, would run from New York City to Pittsburgh, Pennsylvania. That is a long way! Even more exciting is the fact that scientists and explorers haven't even mapped all of it out yet.

With more than 52,000 acres of forests and rivers, Mammoth Cave National Park is home to many endangered species of bats, birds, fish, and

plants. The park was established in 1941 to protect the caves and the habitat surrounding them. With many more miles of cave left to explore, it is almost assured that there will be hundreds of new species of animals discovered in the Mammoth Cave system.

If you are ever in central Kentucky, you should definitely make sure to stop by Mammoth Cave National Park!

Rattlesnakes

There are almost fifty different species of rattlesnakes throughout the Americas. They are named rattlesnakes because of the rattle at the end of their tails that they use as a warning device when threatened.

The beads inside the rattle itself are made up of the same material as the snake's skin. In fact, they *are* the snake's skin. Each time a rattlesnake loses its skin (or "molts"), a new bead is added to the rattle.

The primary foods for rattlesnakes are rodents and other small animals. The rattlesnake uses its fangs to inject venom into the animal, paralyzing it and allowing it to be eaten.

If you are going to go hiking in an area that has rattlesnakes, make sure to wear good, sturdy leather boots and heavy canvas pants. This will help to ensure that a rattlesnake, should you accidentally sneak up on one, will not be able to bite you.

If a rattlesnake is encountered on a trail, keep your distance and make sure the snake has room to move away.

The best thing to do when hiking is to always remain observant!

Crystals

Crystals are some of the most amazing things in the natural world. They come in many different colors and shapes—salt is an example of a crystal that is shaped like a cube. If certain types of crystals are polished, they can become gorgeous gems like emeralds, rubies, and diamonds. Crystals are also incredibly useful—computer chips could not work without them.

But what are crystals, and how do they form? These are difficult questions and won't be easy to

answer. A crystal is a mineral. In fact, most minerals occur naturally as crystals. What makes a crystal a crystal is the way that the tiny particles inside of it (called atoms) are arranged.

Crystals have a very interesting arrangement of atoms. Instead of a random mixture, crystals have atoms made up in a unique pattern. The crystal forces the atoms to link into this special pattern to make the crystal grow. This process repeats over and over and the crystal gets bigger. The way that the crystal looks on the outside is actually a mirror of what the very smallest parts of it look like on the inside. If you want to learn more about crystals, do some research at the library or ask your science teacher.

D0055696